I0591785

# THE MOUNTAIN STOLE MY WIFE

## VICTOR PAUL

This is a work of fiction. Names, characters, places, and incidents either are the product of the author's imagination or are used fictitiously. Any resemblance to actual persons, living or dead, events, or locales is entirely coincidental.

Copyright © 2021 by Victor Paul

All rights reserved. No part of this book may be reproduced or used in any manner without written permission of the copyright owner except for the use of quotations in a book review.

Follow Victor Paul on Instagram: instagram.com/victorpauldomain

First paperback edition February 2021

Book Design by Daniela Owergoor
Typeset by Post Pre-press Group

A catalogue record for this book is available from the National Library of Australia

ISBN 978-0-6450135-3-5 (paperback)
ISBN 978-0-6450135-4-2 (ebook)

*Other books by Victor Paul:*
Chapter Thirteen

# CHAPTER 1

**2006**

*Simon*

My wife is missing, nowhere to be found. I'm the last person other than the forest ranger to have seen her. The mountain spirit might mean something to the people in this town, but back home in Australia it is absolutely ludicrous. No doubt, I am the main suspect. There is nothing I can do to prove my innocence. My wife is missing and I do not have any answers. She went with me to a sacred spot on the mountain that was forbidden; she has been missing ever since. I came out of the spot alone, desperately looking for my wife. I seemed to be blamed for everything from that point on.

### Tony

What do I think of the whole situation? Who knows? Five years with Helen may have caused Simon to push her off the cliff himself. I've known him since high school. There is no way he would hurt anyone, but maybe he reached his limit with her. She controls every aspect of his life. I'm not saying he did it, I'm just saying it's *possible*. I always thought her to be a control freak. Was their relationship as good as it appeared on the outside? I don't know. I asked him what happened on that mountain. All he said was, one minute she was standing on a rock about to take a picture of herself on her phone and the next minute, when he turned around, she was gone. He thought she might be playing a prank or something. But after a few minutes of calling out for her, he realised that she was truly missing. There is this whole thing about this mountain being sacred and people going missing and all. I don't buy it. What happened to her surely has an explanation. I guess the truth will eventually come out. I'm hoping it is not what I think it is. Every man has a breaking point. Did Simon reach his?

### Tegan

Simon messaged me and asked if I had heard from Helen. I was confused at first. I thought they were on a holiday together. I got a call from Simon not long after I responded to his message. He told me Helen had been missing for hours. I told him to go to the police immediately, which he had already done. The first thing I thought was, she must have been kidnapped. She is really pretty and wears designer clothes all the time. I'm so scared for her. I really hope she is found soon. You hear all these horror stories in the news about people held captive. I hope none of this is the case and that my best friend returns to the motel they are staying at. This is certainly not how their wedding anniversary holiday should have started. I feel terrible for them.

### Richard

Simon is responsible for my daughter's disappearance. I have no doubt about that. Why would my son-in-law call me almost two days later to say that Helen is missing? Two days! Was he buying time to cover up his act and come up with a story? I think he's behind all of this. I'm going to get to the bottom of the matter. I've been in the police force for years—something is not right here.

# CHAPTER 2

**2000**

*Simon*

I remember the first time I met Helen. It was at a friend's birthday party. She was a very lively person. I must say, it was pleasant to be around her. She sure gravitates towards adrenaline-pumping stuff—bungee jumping, kitesurfing and all. I, on the other hand, am quite the opposite. Still, I wanted to get her attention. She mentioned skydiving and I thought I should say something at that point.

'I haven't tried skydiving before,' I said.

'It's so fun. You should totally try it.'

'I don't know anyone who would try it with me.'

'I'll go with you. I'm up for doing it again.'

'You will? That's so cool,' I smiled. 'What's your number? I'll hold you to it, you know.'

Her eyes sparkled. She had this cheeky smile, almost as if she knew exactly why I was really asking for her number. She gave it to me anyway. Later, some other guy at the party asked her for it as well, which made me jealous. She's that kind of woman—you can't help but want to know more and more about her. Beautiful hair and a great smile, a great personality—certainly a go-getter. Me? I'm more laidback—hardworking though. I prefer to kick back over a nice movie or a great video game. I'm not an adrenaline junkie.

But hey, opposites attract right?

### Stacy

You know something's up when your workmate comes back from the weekend all smiles. Simon seemed different. You know, us girls can pick these things up. I've been trying to get close to him, but not much is happening other than the usual office interaction. This guy is clearly my type. Neat appearance. Not overly built. Looks great in a suit. Beautiful smile and great overall character. Never heard him swear, and always helping out other team members. I am in love with this guy.

'So, what did you get up to this weekend? You seem happy this morning.'

'Just the usual. Binge drinking, movies and pizzas.'

'Who did you drink with?'

He must have noticed the inquisitive smile on my face which demanded answers.

'Well, it was a friend's party. Nothing really!'

'Come on, you can tell me. You hooked up with someone didn't you?'

'Oh no ... I didn't. Just chilled out and had drinks with friends.'

I was so happy when he said he hadn't, but then he had to ruin it by saying he had met someone. Frankly, I was jealous.

'I might be going skydiving with her,' he said, his cheeks flushing a little.

'*Skydiving?* That's so not you, Simon.'

'I know ... but well ... I just thought I'd give it a try.'

Even after he had said he might be catching up with another girl, I could not muster the courage to ask him to catch up for a coffee with me over the weekend. That would be too obvious. I'll have to wait for another time and then ask him.

### Helen

The first time I met Simon was at a mutual friend's birthday party. He sure is a chatty guy. He seems to know a lot of things. I mean, we were talking about random things at the party and he'd always have some opinion on it. Simon had a neat and sharp appearance—very pleasant to look at. I found out he works for a major bank. He didn't seem like an outdoorsy person, but he did show some appreciation for nature and travel. Somehow, I get the feeling that he might be interested in me. He asked me for my number, but that was more of him wanting to try skydiving with someone. I don't really think I'm his type anyway. He's not the usual kind of guy I date either. Well, I don't mind getting to know a new person in any case. It is the year 2000, so why not!

*Tracy*

My son told me over coffee that he had met someone recently that he would like to get to know better. Simon showed me some pictures of the party and there was a picture of Helen and him together, laughing and having a good time. A candid kind of picture.

'That's a really nice picture of you two.'

'You think so?'

'You almost look like a couple there. Have you asked her out?'

'Well, I haven't got to that point yet.'

'Simon, what are you waiting for? You need to work less, play less video games and stop with all the binge movie-watching. I think you should ask her out. A girl like her will probably get you out there doing stuff.'

We had a good laugh after that and Simon did agree with me. He's doing well with his job and even has a place of his own. He just needs someone in his life now.

### Simon

After a week, I realised I had waited long enough and texted Helen to see if she would like to catch up for coffee. What are the rules of dating in 2000 anyways? She replied, *Catching up for coffee and not for Skydiving?* I kind of got caught there 'cause I wanted to avoid the skydiving as best I could but still get to know her. I replied, *Honestly, I'd really like to get to know you on the ground before we jump out of a plane together.* Anyways, my semi-humorous reply must have got her attention. We messaged back and forth, and she agreed to catch up for coffee with me first. I can't wait to see her again.

### Helen

Simon isn't the typical kind of guy that I would go for. But he seemed really nice at the party. He texted me and asked me out for coffee. I was initially surprised, but I had this feeling from the start that he was interested in me and the skydiving was more of an excuse to get my number. I was right. Cheeky guy. Anyway, it got me thinking about him. Should I give him a chance? Well, I'm not seeing anyone at the moment, and he seems like a genuine guy. I broke up with a real narcissistic guy a few months back. A very tense relationship. My dad thought Matt, my ex, was great for me. He has the occasional beer with Matt and he thinks he's a great guy—the right guy for me. But what does he know?

And besides, what can one harmless coffee with Simon do?

### Tegan

Helen told me she is going to go out with Simon. He sure is striking, judging by the pictures that were taken at the party. He works for the bank; seems like a stable guy, from what Helen tells me. I have to say, he is not one of the usual gym junkie, muscled-up blokes that Helen usually dates. But who knows, she might just be curious to see how the date goes. She seemed quite excited to catch up with him. She asked me for my opinion. *You're single*, I said. *No harm in catching up with someone for coffee.* He sounds like a decent guy. So why not?

### Simon

Who would have guessed that one coffee date would turn into so many others? I guess we had so much to share and talk about. And yes, we did have a skydiving date not too long after our first coffee date. I wouldn't be interested in doing it again though. It really wasn't my thing, but I guess it created some sort of bond between Helen and I. After a few months of seeing each other, I asked her if she wanted to be my girlfriend. Speaking of butterflies in the gut—guys get it too. My feelings were growing stronger and we seemed great together. She agreed. It was a really happy moment in my life.

### Helen

I do feel a strong connection with Simon. We get along really well. I finally feel like I'm in a proper relationship. Time flies when you are having fun, right? Maybe that's why I didn't realise that we have been seeing each other for six months. I wasn't completely taken aback when Simon asked me to be his girlfriend. We were pretty much already functioning like boyfriend and girlfriend—the last two months, especially. I stay over at his apartment occasionally after parties and we spend lots of lazy Sunday afternoons on the couch watching movies. He keeps his apartment really immaculate. I like that about him. He cooks for me quite often as well. I feel everything just flows well with Simon. I said, *Yes, I will be your girlfriend.*

### Anne

I really liked Simon from the time my daughter introduced him to me. Simon is a lovely boy. Well-mannered and respectful. He works for the bank and has a place of his own. He seems to have a good head on his shoulders. Helen seems very comfortable with him too. They have been seeing each other for almost a year now. I've never agreed with Helen on many things but I am sure she made the right decision when she chose to date Simon. I've always been the hard parent, whereas Richard has always been fairly flexible. However, in this particular instance, Richard didn't seem to like Simon very much. I could tell he wasn't impressed. I asked him what the matter was one night after Helen and Simon had joined us for dinner. He simply said he didn't think that Simon was the right fit for Helen. He gave no particular reason, and I couldn't get one out of him either. Is his cop instinct picking up something about Simon that I haven't? I hope not.

*Richard*

On first impression, I just felt that Simon wasn't right for Helen. He's got his life in order, which is good. He's far too soft though. He goes along with whatever Helen says. I prefer her ex-boyfriend, Matt. Matt had more character. Helen needs someone strong like that. I think this is just a phase in her life and this relationship may not go the distance. Might be a short-term thing. I was as polite as possible over dinner.

*Tracy*

Helen is a perfect fit for Simon. I brought up Simon a little soft, you can say. His father left us for another woman when he was just a baby. It truly hurt me at the time. I didn't want Simon to grow up feeling a lack of love because of his father's actions. I kind of spoiled him. He's well-mannered, certainly not rough around the edges. He's a chatty boy who always knows a thing or two about everything. I finally got to meet Helen and Simon for lunch and I instantly liked her. She's a very intelligent woman. A real go-getter too. Reminds me of my younger days when nothing could stop me from making a better life for me and Simon. She's definitely got brains and beauty.

'Helen, get this boy to go out there and experience the world.'

'I know, right. I tell him all the time there's a whole world out there.'

'Helen, just grab his hand and show him.'

'I will. Don't you worry. He's already doing a lot more outdoor stuff now that we're together.'

Such a wonderful woman. I am so happy for the both of them.


*Helen*

Now that we're official, so to speak, Simon wanted to introduce me to his close mate. Simon and I met

Tony for pizza and some drinks at the local pub. First impression, I didn't like Tony. Really up himself. A rude Mr Know-It-All. What an annoying guy. Talking about his gym routines, saying that he's going to open a pizza joint soon and lots of other things, mainly about himself.

'Alright Tony, we've heard enough about you. How do you know Simon?' I said as I interrupted Tony before he could say any more about himself.

'Well, we were high school friends and have been friends ever since. He's a good mate,' he said as he patted Simon on the shoulder.

Fortunately, Simon continued on the conversation to explain how he and Tony met and how their friendship developed. Simon doesn't seem to mind Tony doing most of the talking. He probably thinks he's quite entertaining. I guess because Simon has been friends with Tony for so many years, he's able to put up with him. That's what I took out of everything anyway.

### Tony

When Simon introduced Helen to us, I said straight up, *One word: punching*. He laughed and told me that he knows. She is *hot*. Not that Simon is ugly or anything, he's just a regular bloke. You get my point. Above average with a slim build. He's got an attractive look to him though. It's like his face never ages or something.

The same boyish look that he's had since we were in high school. When we were seventeen, we looked seventeen. Even though we're thirty now, he still looks seventeen. I don't know how that's possible. Must be in his genes or something. He's a really nice guy though. Too nice. I can see Helen walking all over him. He's the kind of bloke that will do anything for his chick. Not me. I won't let a chick tell me what to do.

# CHAPTER 3

**2002**

*Simon*

Helen and I have been seeing each other for two years now. Our connection makes it seem like we've been together a lot longer. I asked her the other day if she was sure that it's only been two years. For me, it feels like twenty. Today was a very nervous day for me. I've hinted on many occasions that I really want her in my life for the long term. I knelt and asked her to marry me. She said yes! I'm determined to make her a very happy woman.

*Stacy*

My heart broke when Simon announced to our work-mates that he was going on annual leave soon as he's going to get married. I mean, what was I thinking? He's been seeing Helen for years now; maybe this is where it was always heading.

'Hey, congrats, I heard the great news,' I said, forcing a smile.

'Thanks. I really appreciate you covering me while I'm on leave.'

'No worries, anything for you, Simon.'

I guess I'd hoped that maybe if things didn't work out between them, he might realise that we could be an item. I mean, we get along great at work. We share lots of the same interests and even enjoy watching the same TV series—well, it's more like I ask Simon what he watches and then I begin watching what he watches— the point is, I enjoy watching the stuff he watches. I can already imagine it: him and I, pizzas, snuggled up on the couch and enjoying a good TV series together. Well, he's not married to her yet. Anything can happen in the meantime. He may realise Helen is not the one for him.

### Helen

I've always got along better with my dad than my mum. But my dad seems disapproving of my relationship with Simon for some reason. My mum likes him a lot and says that she believes I've found the right guy. The one most important decision of my life and I got it right, she says. Thank God. But my dad, he never gave a straight-forward answer as to why he didn't like Simon.

'Come on Dad, what is it about Simon that you don't like?'

'What do you mean? I never said anything bad about him. It's just that I prefer the previous guy.'

'Matt? Oh my God. He was such a narcissist. We didn't really get along. Dad, I love Simon. He's my soulmate.'

I wouldn't go by my dad's standards of choosing a man. Matt is someone I would never settle down with. We had an initial attraction and all, but when it came down to the nuts and bolts of the relationship, it didn't feel right. With Simon, everything just falls into place. My dad didn't say anymore when I said I loved Simon. I guess he got the point—Simon is here to stay in my life.

### Richard

When Helen told me that she's going to marry Simon, I didn't express my disapproval. She's our only child, after all. I did think she would end up with someone different. A tougher guy, like Matt maybe. Simon is too much of a pushover. He simply does everything she says. I met him a few times at family functions and I didn't get along with him too well. Helen asked me before they got married what I honestly thought of Simon. I told her that it's her life at the end of the day. When she said she loved him and he was her soul mate, I held back from saying anything further. I guess the most important thing is that she is safe and happy.

### Anne

I'm overjoyed that Helen is getting married. She found the right person. I feel comfortable knowing that she's marrying Simon. Honestly, if she'd settled down with Matt, I think it would have ended in disaster. Simon and Helen flow well together. They will have a wonderful married life. I have no doubt about that.

### Tony

Getting married? Seriously? That's big news. Simon asked me to be his best man. Seems like yesterday that he introduced Helen to me as his girlfriend and now he's about to call her his wife. I said to him that I'll gladly be his best man. There's no doubt in my mind that he loves Helen. Will they do well together as a couple? I'm not too sure. I honestly thought the relationship would have been short term. I didn't see a chick like Helen staying with Simon, to be honest. Two years? Is that how long they've been together? He's a good bloke and all, but she seemed like she'd have settled down eventually with a different guy. I guess I was wrong. You know what?

I think she likes a pushover. That's exactly what Simon is. A real nice guy, but a pushover.

### Tracy

Simon and Helen are going to make such a lovely married couple. As a mum, I'm so overjoyed for him. I'm glad he's got Helen now to love him and they can start a wonderful journey together. My eyes welled up with tears when he told me that he and Helen are going to get married. Simon, my boy, all grown up and ready to marry and start his life. Where did all the time go? I told him to always look after Helen and make her a happy woman. I told him to not do what his father did to us. That good boy, he gave me a kiss on the cheek and promised to look after her for the rest of his life. Oh, how wonderful! I can't express how happy I am for them both.

### Simon

Helen told her parents that I proposed to her and that we intend to get married. Anne was really excited for us, but Richard didn't seem all that happy. He asked if we'd thought about it carefully since we've only been together for two years. He didn't disapprove, but he didn't seem approving either. Dinner was uncomfortable; his reaction left everything awkward for the rest of the evening. On the drive back home, I asked Helen whether her dad likes me. She just said that he's very protective of his daughter and, being a cop, he's always extra careful with people. I'm not sure if Helen is just saying that to make me feel better. In any case, her dad has always been standoffish with me. There hasn't been much that I've been able to do to make him feel better about me over the past two years.

### Tegan

Oh my God. I can't believe it—Helen's getting married. I'm so excited for her. She's asked me to be her maid of honour. She can count on me for sure. Simon's great for her. I've never seen her so happy in a relationship. There's so much chemistry between them; I wasn't surprised at all to hear that they're getting married.

### Helen

Today is the happiest day of my life. Simon and I got married and things are going to be great from here. I'd like to travel and see many places with Simon. Simon makes me a very happy woman. He bends over backwards for me a lot of the time. I can be very strong-willed, I must say. Simon really is a breath of fresh air compared to all my previous relationships. It feels easy being with him. My dad didn't like that Simon left a lot of the decision-making to me. Hey, happy wife happy life, right? I like that Simon and I really engage in each other's lives. Importantly, I love him.

### Simon

I can't express the happiness I feel today. Helen and I got married. Just before the wedding, Richard had said to me, *I'm giving my daughter's hand to you, make sure you look after her.* Richard and I have never really got along, and I don't think we ever will. He envisioned Helen being with someone other than me from the start and it's become really difficult to change his opinion over the years. I don't know why he sees me as unfit to look after Helen. Helen's a strong woman; she doesn't need me to constantly look out for her. I think Richard is very protective of his daughter as she's the only child. Yes, I do let Helen have her way most of the time, and it's become quite obvious to Richard, who sees it as a weakness. I reassured him that Helen is in good hands and that I'll look after her, but he's obviously not convinced.

# CHAPTER 4

**2006**

*Helen*

I can't believe it, but Simon and I have been married for four years now. I found this place in Indonesia where we can do a forest walk that is beautiful and tranquil. It's apparently some sort of a sacred mountain with beautiful views. There's a spot where you can stand on the edge of the mountain and overlook the surrounding forest and islands. The actual spot is closed to the public because of some local superstition, but I'm going to try and get a picture of me and Simon at that spot. It'll be too beautiful a shot to be missed. Also, before I left for our holiday, I told my mum how happy it made me that she gets along with Simon. My dad, till this day, is either neutral or doesn't get along with him. I've learnt to accept it now—he doesn't see Simon as the ideal partner for me.

In any case, no one knows our relationship better than us. I have lots of romance and fun in my relationship. I do disagree with Simon from time to time, just like any other relationship I suppose, but mostly we get along. He lets me have my way a lot of the time. I can be stubborn at times, but he seems to understand me the most. This is something that's hard to explain to my dad—that Simon is my soulmate, not just my husband. You know what? Someday he will just come to terms with it and we will all get along. I didn't get a chance to speak to my dad before I left. I did tell my mum to let him know that we should all catch up when I'm back. Have a nice lunch or dinner together. Maybe he'll change his opinion if I remind him that Simon and I have been married for four years now.

### Simon

It's really an amazing feeling to know that Helen and I have been married for four years now. I'm so excited to celebrate it with her. She's organised a trip to a remote part of Indonesia, a few hours from Bali in a tranquil mountainous area. Helen's looking forward to it. There's also a part on the mountain that overlooks the sea and the surrounding islands, but that spot has been closed for years. Helen wants to go and see it for herself. I'm not too sure about entering a place that's closed to the public. In any case, I simply want to enjoy myself and have a getaway with her. We haven't had a holiday for a while now. It'd be nice to have some time away for ourselves, away from work, and to celebrate our wedding anniversary.

### *Art*

The Kula Mountain has a tranquil forest walk that lots of tourists like to take. On both sides of the mountain trail lays a dense forest. We have signboards to advise the tourists to stick to the trail. Beyond the mountains and the forest is the powerful sea and there's a spot which has been closed for years due to superstition and several mishaps. It's the best spot to view the ocean below and the vast forest, but several people have gone missing entering that spot. It's away from the regular trail as well. The local authorities closed it several years ago now. The locals believe that the mountain spirit resides there and it's a sacred spot not to be entered by any ordinary person. My family have been the caretakers and rangers of this area for decades. I respect the beliefs of the people in my town. The spot is dangerous—many people try to step onto the loose rocks to gain a grand view of the island. If they fall off the edge of the cliff, they will fall many feet into the sea, which has strong currents. The sea is also rumoured to be infested with sharks. There's literally no chance of survival.

## Kran

During the tourist season, my boys and I go down to the Kula Mountain town area to discreetly sell *ganja*, or what the Westerners call 'marijuana'. We hang around the motels where these Westerners stay and try to get their attention when they come out of their motels. My boys and I live in the outskirts of the town, not too far from the Kula Mountain. The police chief has been trying to catch me and my boys out for years, but maybe he doesn't want to either, as long as we don't come into town too often or get spotted selling marijuana openly. I take the risk because these foreigners pay five to ten times more for the drugs than the locals. It is good money. The laws in Indonesia are strict if we get caught. It is the death penalty for drug traffickers like me. My father used to run the gang when I was young. He died of a heroin overdose when I was in my late teens. I've taken over the gang as their leader. I'm known for my temper and I'm generally regarded by the townspeople as a dangerous guy. They stay out of my way. The police chief is still investigating a murder that took place when my boys and I were in town a few months back. Some of the local townsmen come to the outskirts and spend a huge amount of their pay smoking our drugs and drinking the illegal alcohol we brew. We sell cheap contraband cigarettes to them as well. There're a few food stalls for them to eat at when they come out here. Then, once their pockets are empty, they go back to their families with very little money for the month.

### Budiwati

My father named me Budiwati, meaning *the wise one*. The mountain and forest might be a tourist attraction to foreigners, however, to most people here, it is a sacred place. My son, Art, is the caretaker of this forest and sacred mountain. There's a particular spot on the mountain which is really dangerous for people to go to. That's where the mountain spirit is. Most who have gone there have not returned. I remember when I was a young girl, about nine years old, my father and I were taking a walk along the forest trail. He liked to feed the monkeys and leave offerings for the mountain once a month. The air was so fresh; I could smell all kinds of flowers and plants growing in the forest.

My father was busy feeding the monkeys when I heard a powerful voice calling to me from the sacred spot. My father had warned me never to go there; I'm not sure to this day why I decided to run straight for it. I came across the most beautiful part of the mountain where there was a large rock. I climbed my way onto it. I could see the majestic mountains and forest all around.

The surrounding islands were so beautiful. A huge smile broke out across my face and I remembered feeling this great sense of peace and happiness.

Then, suddenly, I looked down and saw the vast angry seas roaring below, with violent waves smashing against the rocks. Fear struck me. *Budiwati!* I heard my father shout in the loudest voice. I turned around and saw him at the entrance of the sacred spot, his eyes filled with fear. I began to shake as a huge gust of wind knocked against my back with a powerful force. I fell onto the ground below from the high rock. My father rushed to pick me up and asked if I was okay. I nodded my head as he hurriedly carried me away. After that incident, I told my father that I could hear the voice of the mountain spirit. He told me that if I could hear the mountain spirit, I would be the next spiritual woman after he was gone, tasked with carrying on the tradition. And so it has been since he left.

### Helen

I woke up in the morning in a cold sweat. I knew it had something to do with the mountain that we're heading to today. Simon looked concerned as I jolted awake.

'Are you alright?'

'I'm fine. Just a bad dream ... Something to do with the mountain. It's nothing.'

'Helen, the spot that you're talking about—a local has warned me that it's a sacred spot. It's closed to the public.'

I know Simon all too well; he doesn't like anything that's risky. 'We'll just go in and out of this so-called forbidden spot, get a couple of pictures of it and leave. What's the big deal?'

'You said you had a bad dream about the mountain. Don't you think it might be a sign—'

'Simon, you know I'm still going to go to that spot, right? I'm not going to let a dream or some town superstition stop me.'

I knew Simon was concerned, but sometimes he needs a push to take risks.

I can't remember everything that happened in that dream. It's one of those dreams where you know you had a bad dream but forget most of the details as soon as you wake up. I don't want to come all the way out here and not see that spot. Simon and I will go for a hike in the forest and then we'll head to the spot on the mountain. I do not believe in their superstitions at all and I'll not let them deter me from enjoying this experience.

### Kran

I spotted a couple coming out of the town's motel where most of the tourists stay this time of year. The woman was very pretty. I couldn't stop staring at her. I only stopped when her man pulled her closer and started walking away from me. I smoked the last of my cigarette and threw it to the ground, trying to get their attention. The woman was wearing expensive jewellery. Their clothes didn't look cheap either. I was sure this was a wealthy young couple.

'Marijuana! Marijuana!' I said as I walked closer, just loud enough for them to hear me.

'I don't smoke,' said the man, waving me away.

'Maybe she smokes marijuana,' I said, eyeing the beautiful woman from head to toe with a broad smile.

She yelled at me, telling me that neither of them smokes marijuana before rudely walking away. I was really angry. How dare she talk to me like that! Doesn't she know who I am? I am Kran. People in this town know my reputation and fear me. She'd better watch out.

### Helen

Simon and I set out for Kula Mountain after breakfast and ran into an unsavoury character as we came out of the motel. The man was covered in tattoos and was staring me down in an unpleasant way as Simon and I walked past him. Simon pulled me closer as he started walking towards us. As if Simon's response to him wasn't good enough, he was trying to get *me* to buy it from him. I'd already had a poor start, waking up from a bad dream, and this guy kind of annoyed me further. I lashed out, asking him to go away. He got the message and I think I kind of scared him away. He seemed very different to the other people in this town. Most of them are respectful and pleasant. This guy had a very bad aura. All I wanted to do was have a nice peaceful forest walk and relax.

Simon tried to convince me that we should respect the town's beliefs and avoid the sacred place. I told him that I've come too far to not go to that spot. I promised him we won't stay there too long. I'll get a couple of scenic photos and some nice pictures of us. I reminded him that it's our wedding anniversary and he's got to be extra nice to me. I think that finally got Simon to agree to go. I'm so excited to see this place.

### Simon

As I ran out, shouting Helen's name, I spotted the forest ranger, Art. He had seen us earlier and told us not to enter the closed spot, but we went against his warning. I asked him if he'd seen the woman who was with me earlier. He said no. I panicked. I've been calling her mobile phone and it appears to be switched off or something—maybe it's the reception in the area. He told me that the spot we entered was a sacred and forbidden spot. There have been incidents of missing persons over the years, which is why the place was closed to the public. I told him that all Helen wanted to do was stand on top of that rock and take a picture. He shook his head at me but told me he would help me look for her. The strong winds were howling loudly in my ears, as they had been from the time Helen and I entered the sacred spot. I initially thought Helen was playing a prank and wanted to scare me. I realised minutes later that she was really missing. Art tells me that there's a strong superstition surrounding the mountain spirit. But I would be ridiculed if I told anyone back home that the mountain stole my wife. I don't believe in mountain spirits. I think she could've been kidnapped by some locals for ransom money. I will get to the bottom of this. She is somewhere on this island; I can feel it.

### Sawan

These Westerners don't understand that we have super-stitions that go way back to our great, great grandfathers. As a police chief do I believe in superstition? Of course. There are some things that cannot be explained, and I choose to leave it that way. I know that the mountain spirit took his wife away. She went to a spot that was sacred where there was a sign that clearly said *no entry*, and this obviously angered the mountain spirit. Now she is gone forever. People have been going missing for years at that spot. What can we do? Her husband came to the station and reported his missing wife. I told him to go back to the motel and wait for her in case she finds her way back there. I will still have to conduct investigations to locate this missing Westerner. You know, I'm not getting paid enough to do this job. Now this case will be the top priority and it really is a pain, I tell you. But what can I do? I need to feed my wife and four kids.

### Art

I was questioned by the police chief about the missing Western woman. I can't believe that I'm sitting in a police station being questioned about a missing person. Am I a suspect just because I'm the last to have seen them going into the forbidden area? This is rubbish. They know me and my family—we have been the rangers of this forest for years. I told the police chief, Sawan, that he knows me and my family, and we do not have anything to do with a missing person. He said he had no choice; due to the nature of a missing foreigner, everyone involved and every possible suspect must be interrogated. I told Sawan what I knew.

'Sawan, I told that couple not to go in and that's the last I saw of them.'

'Art, I still have to take statements and make a report,' said Sawan with a sigh. 'Did they say anything to you?'

'I think the couple understood that they were not supposed to enter that area.'

'Here, have some coffee. The problem is that the missing person is a foreigner,' said Sawan as he pushed a mug towards me.

'Sawan, what do you want me to do? I've already told you what I know.'

My job is on the line. There is a suspicion that the man's wife might have been kidnapped. My family have been responsible for this sacred forest for many years and I clearly told the couple that the spot was forbidden. I didn't give them a full explanation; I just told them that place is closed and carried on with my usual routine checks. Who would've thought all of this would happen?

### Kran

Sawan spotted me in town and took me into the station to question me. Fortunately, it was my boys that had all the marijuana on them. I was busy following some tourist, trying to push the drugs and then signalling my boys to sell to whoever wanted it.

'Kran, there is a missing tourist and you and your boys are in town,' said Sawan as he leaned forward from his desk and stared me in the eye.

The guilt in my eyes and the sweat pouring down my face wasn't helping. I kept my cool as far as possible.

'Sawan, you want to blame me for everything! You're already investigating me for murder and now you're saying I'm responsible for a missing tourist?'

Sawan didn't respond for a while. 'So, what are you and your boys doing in town today?'

'We came to get groceries for the food stalls. They're running out of items.'

'Kran, don't play games with me!' shouted Sawan as he stood up from his chair and adjusted his police belt, his face stern.

'Sawan, you have known me for many years. Why would I be involved in kidnapping a tourist?'

'Because my sources tell me that business at your so-called food stalls is not doing too well. My sources also told me that the guy who was murdered a few weeks ago owed you a lot of money,' said Sawan, staring long and hard at me.

He was cornering me. 'Sawan, I don't know anything, and you can't just detain me here for no reason.'

Sawan knew he had nothing on me. After a while, he released me from the police station. He warned me that he'll be watching me and my boys closely. Hey, these tourists who come here have lots of money. I don't see anything wrong with a tourist being held for ransom.

### Simon

The police chief was really helpful, saying *don't worry we'll do all we can to find her*. He's had his sources out on the street to see if she was kidnapped. It's been two days since Helen went missing and it's killing me inside not knowing where she is. I do not accept the theory that the mountain spirit has stolen my wife. That is the most ludicrous thing I've ever heard in my life. They've questioned the forest ranger and believe he may be a possible suspect. I'm just a tourist in this town and have to rely on the police chief to find my wife. The people of the town hardly speak English and don't seem to want to get involved. I really am at my wits' end.

### Richard

Being a police officer, you can never be too sure of people. I've been in the force for so many years; I've seen it all. Honestly, when I got the call from Simon, I suspected that he had something to do with Helen's disappearance. It just didn't seem right.

'You're telling us this after *two days?*'

'I didn't know what to do. I was hoping she'd turn up after a day or so as the police and local rangers are searching for her. I've been searching for her too.'

'You should've called us as soon as she went missing. I'm coming to Indonesia to find my daughter!'

Why would he call us a full two days later? If she was kidnapped by some local, wouldn't they have made some sort of contact by now? Unless Simon has something to do with her disappearance. I will get to the bottom of this.

## Anne

When we got the call that Helen has been missing for two days, my heart sank. I imagined the worst. *Kidnapped* was the first thing that came to my mind. It is a foreign country and with everything that's been happening in the world, I could not imagine that she was simply lost in the forest. Richard kept saying Simon had something to do with it and that he didn't trust him.

'You're not suggesting that Simon ...?'

'I don't trust him, and I've never liked him. I'm going to get to the bottom of this!'

I couldn't convince Richard to let me go with him to Indonesia. When he gets into that mode, there is no compromise; it's Richard's way or the highway. The situation was already terrible and I didn't want to create even more tension. I just cried and asked him to bring our daughter back home safe.

## Simon

I had no choice but to call my in-laws after two days and tell them that Helen is missing. Richard was really angry over the phone and demanded to know how something like this could happen. He said he's coming to Indonesia to join the search for her. Anne was more sympathetic and asked more about exactly what had happened. I gave her all the details that I knew and I could hear her crying over the phone. She said Helen was her only child and to please find her and bring her back. I said I would surely do my best.

### Richard

When I got to Indonesia and caught up with Simon, I was fuming with anger. I grabbed him by his shirt and demanded answers. No more *Helen is missing and I don't know where she is.*

'Richard calm down.'

'Don't tell me what to do.'

I finally released my grip on his shirt. He took me to the spot where Helen went missing after persuading the forest ranger—Artie, or whatever his name is—to let us through. I did my own investigations and tried to reconstruct the moment she went missing. Simon claimed he was distracted and was looking in the opposite direction before she evaporated into thin air.

'You said this is a forbidden area and only two of you entered the place. Why are there so many footprints on the sand?'

'I don't know. I went back and forth looking for her and the forest ranger and I were also looking for her. Could be all our footprints?'

'Were you that stupid to come here when it clearly says "no entry"?'

'Look Richard, I told Helen not to, but she ignored me.'

I was done talking to Simon. I'm going straight to the police chief and we're going to investigate what happened to my daughter.

### Sawan

The missing girl's father was telling me how to do my job. I understand his anger and frustration—I've got two daughters of my own, so I know the feeling. But coming over to the station and saying that we're sitting around doing nothing really made me angry.

'Sir, we're doing our best. What more do you want from us?'

'I want you to have your team out there looking for her. She could've been kidnapped.'

I spoke to some of the local outlaws; clearly, she had not been kidnapped. No one was asking for ransom money. She went to a sacred spot and now she is missing. This has happened so many times. Why would it change just because his daughter went there? How am

I to explain this to him? Just to calm him down, I got up from my seat and said I was heading out to speak to someone. I told him that he should continue searching for Helen with his son-in-law. I assured him that if my team or I heard anything, we would let him or Simon know immediately. What a pain this whole situation is for everyone!

## *Art*

I was initially very angry with Simon; he had caused me so much trouble and had even got me on the suspect list. However, as he started to speak more to me whilst we searched for his wife, I realised that he's a good guy. I feel sorry for him. What if my wife Suri went missing? He asked me more about the forbidden area. I told him that the place has been closed to the public for years. I told him a story of a boy who went missing on the mountain. I don't know why I did it; I just wanted to tell a story from when my father was the forest ranger. A boy took off up the mountain and went missing. He was last seen by the other kids entering the sacred spot. His parents searched the forest for a couple of days, calling out his name, and they never found him. They then decided to seek out my mother for some advice. They later brought some offerings and left them at the entrance to the sacred area, as advised by my mother.

They were hoping the mountain spirit would give them back their son.

'So, what happened?' asked Simon.

'Well, believe it or not, the boy returned the very next day.'

'Is this a true story?'

'It is. The boy looked frightened and hardly spoke for days.'

'The mountain spirit gave the boy back? How does your mother know these things?'

'My mother is the local spiritual woman of this town.'

Simon went really silent after that.

He finally spoke just as we were approaching my house for dinner.

'Do you think that the mountain spirit will return my wife?'

'Simon—'

'Can you ask your mother to help me?'

He looked desperate and sad. The boy that went missing returned after three days. He might have got lost in the forest and found his way back or the mountain spirit might have returned him. Who knows? Simon's wife has been gone for a whole week now. I doubt she will be returning. I wish I had not told him the story now, because you know what? I think the boy got lost in the forest. If I said that to the townspeople, they would be so angry with me. So I just don't say anything. Still, I felt obligated to ask my mother about Simon's request.

At the large stone area where his wife went missing, you can see the sea below. I've been told that this is the eye of the mountain. Those who stare into it can be lost forever. This is the superstition of the town.

## Budiwati

It's really heartbreaking to hear after so many years that the mountain spirit has taken someone again. The last incident I remember was when my husband was the forest ranger. A woman had gone to the exact spot and never returned. Art has told me there's a sign to prevent people from entering the sacred spot. I can't understand why someone would do it anyway. When Art came back home, he told me that Simon asked if the mountain spirit will return his wife. The man seems desperate for answers. I feel it is my duty to help him. I'm hoping I'll get the same sign I got many years ago about the missing boy. Maybe a peace offering to the mountain could bring her back. There are many others who've gone missing and never returned. Honestly, the missing boy's parents were very fortunate that the mountain spirit returned him. When the boy was found, he was covered in dirt and soil. He kept saying he was lost until he saw a bright light that led him out to the trail. The mountain spirit must have kept him somewhere as punishment for entering the sacred spot but later decided to return him.

### Simon

Budiwati looked at me blankly while waiting for Art to translate our conversation. She closed her eyes, as if retreating into a strange world. Those sixty seconds were the longest seconds of my life. I wanted her to open her eyes and say the words that I so desperately needed to hear. Art waited patiently for his mother's response. As she opened her eyes, tears poured from them like a cup overfilled with water. My heart sank. She said something to Art that I knew he wasn't translating back fully; he touched me on the shoulder and kept saying *don't worry*. Budiwati's tears continued to flow and I could no longer hold it together. I wept bitterly and, like a mother stretching out her arms to comfort her own son, she stretched out her arms to me. I hugged her and wept uncontrollably. What was I thinking anyway? My wife is missing, and I had clung to every hope of her coming back to me, even if it was meant believing in the mountain spirit.

### Budiwati

I can't speak good English; Art normally translates when Simon speaks to me. Simon asked me if the mountain spirit would return his wife. I felt so sorry for the young man. I understood from Art that Simon and his wife had come to our town to celebrate their wedding anniversary. Art translated what he had said and I closed my eyes to see if I could summon any sign from the mountain spirit. I wish I'd seen a vision of his wife walking back to him from the forbidden area. I wish the voice of the mountain would have demanded offerings near the entrance of the forbidden spot to release his wife. Instead, I saw a figure of a woman fading into the unknown darkness. I knew then that the mountain spirit was not willing to give her back. My sadness was so deep that when I opened my eyes, tears streamed down my face. Simon broke down and started crying too. I stretched out my arms to give him a hug and comfort him as if he were my own son.

### *Anne*

The phone call from Richard broke my heart. He had searched for almost a week and there was simply no trace of her. Helen is nowhere to be found. Our daughter is gone. Our one and only child. Gone, just like that. Richard said he would discuss it when he comes back; he didn't want to talk any further over the phone. I had so many questions and no answers. How did this happen? Richard returned home from Indonesia and it was all bad news. Full investigations were underway and the police have been involved. I'm not sure why they entered an area so dangerous. Richard said briefly that there is this thing about the mountain spirit and that people go missing when they enter that spot. I'm so confused. What has all this superstition got to do with our daughter? I'm so lost.

# CHAPTER 5

**2007**

*Simon*

Most people tried their best to comfort me with words. But the pain of losing my beloved Helen could not be numbed by talking. I struggled to get through each day. The thoughts in my head were the worst. I ended up drinking almost every night. Sleepless nights. I turned up late for work frequently and made mistakes. Fortunately, most people were quite helpful in covering me. Small things that remind me of Helen set me off. Her voice is always in my head.

*Tony*

Simon's not the same guy since Helen's disappearance. Look, everyone wants to sugar-coat the situation. I think she's dead. I think Helen fell off the cliff whilst trying to take a photo. Who would expect such a tragic thing to happen? No one. But it did. Simon's more reserved now and catch-ups with him are fairly short; he doesn't want to hang out much. I tried my best to tell him to move on, but there is only so much you can do as a mate.

### Richard

I don't want to have anything to do with Simon. He lost our only precious daughter. He was supposed to look after her. The least that I expected from him was to keep her safe. My daughter is missing, and no one is able to find her. Yes, I do blame him and hold him responsible for what has happened. I'm in the police force and we are all held responsible for our actions. Is he responsible for everything that has happened? Of course he is!

### Anne

We came to accept that Helen had passed away after months of investigations. The investigations proved no foul play, and the most likely explanation for Helen's disappearance is that she had fallen off the cliff into the sea while trying to take a picture. They believe a body could not be found as the sea below is infested with sharks. She would've had a close to zero chance of survival given that she most likely sustained a terrible injury from the fall. Her phone was never recovered. There was also the dreadful *The Mountain Stole Helen* theory, which Richard and I found completely ridiculous. How this could even be factored into the investigations was beyond me. They now have more signs and barricades to prevent people from entering the area. We lost our daughter due to the negligence of these townspeople. They should have had more signs and barricades to prevent entry in the first place. Whatever the case is, none of my frustration is going to bring my daughter back. This is a pain that I will have to live with.

### Simon

Stacy's been really pleasant after all that has happened. She covered a huge chunk of my workload while I was away. I couldn't be more thankful. She's been staying back a lot in the office as well. I do offer to buy her dinner at times to show my gratitude. Then I get back home, and my reality and emptiness hits me. The nights are really hard. Helen's family has decided to organise a funeral in remembrance of Helen. I agreed to go ahead with it, although it pained me inside to even consider that she might be dead. Anne told me at the funeral that she would also appreciate it if I cut ties with the family as she didn't want to upset Richard. Richard had clearly told her to say this because I could see that it's not what Anne wanted. It was painful to hear, but I understood where my in-laws were coming from. I blame myself for allowing Helen and I to enter a forbidden area. Helen has always been adventurous, and it's very hard to explain to my in-laws that I did try to stop her but she wouldn't listen. I simply accepted all the blame for her disappearance. I got home from the funeral and felt such heaviness in my heart. I still can't come to terms with the fact that she is gone; I still believe that she is somewhere on that island. I can feel it strongly in my heart. Maybe the mountain spirit did take her. If that's the case, it can return my wife back to me—or maybe that's the bottle of whiskey talking.

### Stacy

It's been almost a year since Simon lost his wife. What really happened to her, no one really knows. We just know that she's classified as a missing person. I really felt sad for his loss but I thought he would have moved on by now. He clearly hasn't. I was his workmate even before he was married to Helen. I had a crush on him then and I still have a crush on him now. In fact, my feelings for him have become stronger. I finally decided to tell him, but he clearly wasn't interested in a new relationship and hadn't got over Helen. As much as I respected his feelings, I was really upset that he did not reciprocate mine. After I had opened up to him and told him that I would like to see him outside of work, he politely declined. I think maybe it's time for me to move on and consider someone else. Gareth at our workplace has been showing a lot of interest in me. I might give him a chance. Still, I'm hoping Simon might change his mind eventually.

*Sawan*

The mountain spirit claims another life. After almost a year of investigations, we've had to close the file. I've used every resource I have to try and locate his missing wife. There are no kidnappers. No ransom and no dead body. I even spoke to a few local outlaws and asked them if they had seen or heard anything—but nothing. Just a missing person lost to the mountain spirit. I have done my job and my superiors have agreed to close the file and classify it as *unresolved*. I've been heavily overworked and it's caused me a lot of stress. There was a lot of pressure to find this one, especially since she was a foreigner. I think the mountain spirit took her away. People who go to the forbidden area have gone missing before. I'm not sure why it didn't take Simon away. That remains a mystery.

*Richard*

After the funeral, I became more reserved. I never brought up Helen with Anne or anyone else. I buried all my hurt and even when Helen was mentioned, I simply said nothing. She has gone to a better place and talking about her is not going to do anyone any good. I'm glad Anne has respected my decision to cut ties with Simon as I don't want to be reminded that we have lost Helen. I love my daughter and how I choose to deal with it is my business.

*Anne*

After Helen's funeral, my marriage entered a stalemate. Richard took up more duties at the police station and always returned home late. Richard was a stern, straightforward guy when I married him, but he used to do small romantic things that I loved. He used to leave fresh flowers on the breakfast table for me when he got back from his rotational night-shift duties. He would never go to bed before making me a cup of coffee and giving me a kiss. All that has changed. Now he comes home and goes straight to bed. I don't know what I should do. I sometimes wonder if he still loves me. I lost my daughter; I don't want to lose my husband as well.

# CHAPTER 6

**2011**

*Simon*

I went to the doctor today and received some bad news. Honestly, it didn't concern me too much. The anniversary of Helen's disappearance is coming soon, and I have to make it to Indonesia to pay my respects. I'm looking forward to it, as I do every year. I feel that this year something different is going to happen.

*Anne*

Today marks five years since our daughter left us. I find it hard to comprehend that she is gone. As a mother, it's hard to let go. I do feel bad that Richard ended our relationship with Simon. He was the one person who could make me feel closer to my daughter. I understand that she's gone, but the heart doesn't understand these things and we do what we need to do to move on. Richard seems to have taken a different approach to all that has happened. He doesn't talk about it much—to me or anyone else. I've been tempted to call Simon and speak with him so many times. Just normal things about him and Helen which might have made me feel closer to my long-lost daughter. I refrained, as I knew it would greatly upset Richard and there's been enough pain in the family already. I came out of the shopping centre today, and as I was about to start the car I broke down and cried uncontrollably at the thought of her absence. The emotions simply spilled out of me.

### Stacy

I've been married to Gareth for a year now. I know for sure that Gareth loves me. I can see it in his eyes. Do I love Gareth? That's really hard to answer, but I do have strong feelings for him and I do take my relationship with him seriously. It's hard to understand a woman's heart. I got a job offer and lost touch with Simon after leaving the bank. Gareth moved to a different division. I don't ask Gareth about Simon as he suspects that I used to have a thing for him. I never verbalised it and he never asked, but somehow he knew I've had eyes for Simon in the past. My marriage with Gareth is going great. Do I think of Simon from time to time? Of course

I do! I'd never say it to Gareth though. It would upset him. I just hope Simon is well.

## Budiwati

Art told me that Simon is coming to visit us in a few weeks' time. Simon doesn't seem to be okay. He smiles, talks to us politely and puts on a happy face, but there is a deep sadness buried within him. I asked Art why he doesn't just move on and remarry so that he at least has some companionship. Art tells me Simon doesn't want to. Maybe he's happy with the memories of Helen and that is enough for him. I wonder who looks after him when he goes back to Australia. When he comes here, we look after him like he is family. I treat him like another son. Art tells me that Simon didn't get good news from the doctor about his health. I hope when he visits us he can rest, feel better and maybe get well soon. Time is not on my side and old age has caught up with me. I told Art to always look out for him, even when I'm gone. I don't know how much longer I'll be around.

## Art

Simon seemed happy in a strange way and was dressed in a suit when he came to visit his wife's grave. Something was different about him. I asked him what the doctors had said and he told me the results were not good but he'd be fine. I presumed that although the news wasn't good, he should be fine with treatment. We both went to visit his wife's grave and left some flowers. I opened the gates to let Simon into the sacred area where he normally spends some time. As I let him in, I mentioned that I really liked his suit and that's when he said something that made me feel uncomfortable: it was the same suit he wore on his wedding day. I wasn't sure if I'd made a mistake in opening the gates this time. I told him that I would see him in an hour and he responded how he normally would: with a nod and a wave. I'm taking a bit of a chance here. I could get into a lot of trouble if anything goes wrong.

### *Tony*

My second marriage has come to an end before it even started. Apparently I am a heartless guy and I don't care enough. I am the most passionate guy. Ask my staff, they will tell you how good a boss I am. Anyway, I'm happy to get her out of my life. The hard part was asking my dad to help me out again 'cause I'm not willing to lose the restaurant. What are the odds, you get married twice and they both fail! I'm quite over relationships at this point. As for Simon, I think he lost all the happiness in his life after Helen. If I could give Simon some advice – it would be that women aren't worth the heartache. I tried to get him to come to the gym with me over the weekends since he claims he's busy on weekdays with work. He has turned to alcohol a lot over the years to deal with his emotions. I've suggested that he go into some sort of therapy to help him cope, but it all seems to fall onto deaf ears. I've got my own problems as well. What else can I do? You can only bring the horse to the water right?

### Simon

This is my fifth visit to my wife's grave. The doctors have advised me that I shouldn't travel due to my health condition. Well, I still had to pay my respects, regardless of what the doctor said. I decided to wear the suit I got married in. I got myself a nice haircut as well; I wanted to look my best. I had a feeling that this trip was going to be special. She may have been gone for five years now, but she's been living in my heart and mind every day. As I was walking with Art toward Helen's grave, I felt a very sharp pain near my abdomen. I thought of stopping to rest, but since I was so close to the grave, I continued walking. I didn't want to show Art any signs of my pain. I feared he would take me back to his place to rest. Art usually opens the chained gates to the sacred spot for me and I sit on the rock and look into what the locals call 'the eye of the mountain'. I sometimes wish the mountain spirit would take me away as it did Helen, but this has never happened.

I went to the rock and could see the sun sitting low in the sky, about to descend. The pain in my abdomen was unbearable but I wouldn't miss being here today for the world. For the past few years, I've had this feeling that I'm getting closer to seeing Helen. Is the mountain going to return my wife or will she miraculously appear one day in the very spot she went missing? I don't know. Your mind starts to play games as the years go on. Everyone around you tells you to move on and that your missing wife will not return. And the pep talks I've got over the years from so many different people around me ... I don't even want to get into it. But I never gave up. I just want her back, to be reunited with her. As I sat on the rock, the pain worsened and I was overcome by the need to lie down. That's when I felt someone touch me on the shoulder. At first I thought it might be Art, back from his routine walk. Then I heard Helen's voice whisper, *Simon*.

I looked up and it was her! When she said my name, I was speechless. I wanted to ask her everything and tell her everything. Where should I start? I choked on my own words and my lips were shaking. The tears were streaming down my face and I wiped at them desperately so that they wouldn't blur my vision of her.

She sat beside me and told me not to cry. She was here now. I told her she'd been gone for a very long time and I missed her. I just couldn't stop crying. *Don't you ever leave me like that again, Helen*, I said to her. She said she was not going anywhere and would be here to stay. She wiped the tears from my face. I held her hands tightly and looked at her. I felt her comforting kiss on my lips. All my pain started to slowly disappear. She stood up and took my hands, encouraging me to rise. I got up and we walked towards the sun, hand in hand.

## *Art*

I was troubled as I went for my routine checks around the forest. I was walking faster than usual and couldn't wait to get back to the gates. I took half the time I normally take and came into the forbidden area as fast as I could. I found Simon sitting on the rock and breathed a sigh of relief. It seemed like he was speaking to someone; he was saying something, but I couldn't quite catch it from such a distance. I waited for a while as I didn't want to interrupt him. The sun was beginning to set. He stretched out his right hand. At that point, I understood that he was speaking to his long-lost-wife's spirit. I waited for him, hoping that when he was done, he would stand up and walk back; it would be dark soon. Instead, his body fell slowly to its side. I ran towards the rock and shook him. He had passed away. He was finally reunited with his Helen.

### Anne

I didn't tell Richard about the incident at the shopping centre. It's not like he would care anyway, these days. Later that day, I got a call from Simon's mum. She told me that Simon had passed away. I was in complete shock.

'What do you mean?'

'He's gone, he's dead.'

'Tracy, what happened?'

'He was in the final stages of his cancer and no one knew about it. Simon goes to Indonesia every year to visit Helen at that spot. He passed away while he was there. I got a call from the forest ranger.'

It was heartbreaking. I was speechless. I was completely unaware that Simon had been going back to the spot where our daughter went missing. When the call ended, I broke down.

### Art

Apparently, Simon had written in his will that he would like to be buried next to the empty grave of his wife. His final wishes were fortunately respected by his mother, and the townspeople who had come to know him over the years helped in making a grave for him. My wife and I visit his grave every now and then and leave flowers. Simon is a brother of mine that I will never forget. I'm sure he is in a happy place now.

# EPILOGUE

Anne moved out and separated from Richard in 2011. That same year she made a trip to Indonesia to visit Helen and Simon's grave. In 2012, she filed for divorce and cut her ties with Richard completely. She has not heard from Richard since.

Richard was called into the Secret Service in 2011, just after his separation. In 2012, after his official divorce settlement, he took up a classified overseas mission. His current whereabouts are unknown.

Stacy remains married to Gareth. She is expecting her second child, a boy. She eventually found out about the death of Simon. After much dispute with Gareth, Stacy found a way to convince him to name their second son Simon.

Tegan joined the police force and currently works in a unit that specialises in missing persons.

Sawan retired and a new police chief took over a stack of paperwork and backlogs. There was a section in the filing cabinet relating to the forbidden area of the mountain. There were a total of ninety reported cases in which people were last seen going to the forbidden zone and had never returned. The cases were closed with the description *unresolved*. Helen's name was amongst those files. Sawan advised the new police chief, who came from a different part of the country, to leave those cases alone and, importantly, not to enter the sacred spot. The new police chief, contrary to what Sawan had said, went to the sacred spot after his shift that evening. He had boasted to the junior staff that he didn't believe in superstition or spirits. He is currently classified as a missing person. Sawan had to return to work for an additional month whilst a replacement police chief was being assigned to the town.

Kran was arrested in 2011 for possession and trafficking of marijuana. The death penalty was imposed on him due to the volume of drugs that he was caught with. He was executed the year following his arrest.

Art continued to work as the forest ranger and has been training his son to take over. He is happily married and intends to pass on his duties to his eldest son when he retires to continue the family tradition of caretaking.

Tony has been single since his second divorce. He spends most of his days at the restaurant. Tony has yet to visit Simon's grave in Indonesia.

Tracy continued to live on with the memories of Simon and Helen. Shortly after Simon's death, she went to Simon's apartment to collect his belongings. She found several empty whiskey bottles lying around the apartment. She also found countless notes and letters addressed to Helen expressing just how much he missed her.

Budiwati passed away peacefully in 2013. She was the town's last known spiritual woman. The superstition of the mountain spirit and its sacred spot continues on for many of the townspeople.

www.ingramcontent.com/pod-product-compliance
Lightning Source LLC
Chambersburg PA
CBHW070359120726
47909CB00008B/2913